A Non-Traditional Children's Book

The

Journey

South

"A Children's Story"

by
Clarence A Harris

Dedication

This book is dedicated to my family, without whom I would not have achieved what I have – in life and love. To my daughters, Paris Stanton and A'Nijah Harris, this is mainly dedicated to you because this shows you that your beginning does not have to be your end. In school, I was not the book smart guy nor the praised athlete. In fact, I barely graduated high school at 20 years old. Yeah, you guessed it right, I failed a couple of grades. Today I sit here as a retired (20 years) military veteran who does not have to work ever again, a college graduate with a Master's degree, and a published author of not one but two books with more on the way. So remember, "It's not how you start the race; it's how you finish it." I love you and thank you for being my girls

Acknowledgment

I would like to thank God for instilling into me a drive and determination that don't allow me to stop, sit down, and be quiet. To my family, I want to thank you for your support through my bad times and through my good times. Without you, none of what I do or have done would be possible.

Throughout my military career and now my civilian life, you have always been there for me. I want you to know that I will always aspire to be the best and do my best to make you proud.

I will go to the ends of the earth to ensure your security. Making you proud of me will always be the ultimate high in my life!

About the Author

Clarence Alvin Harris is a retired Army Soldier (Army Veteran/Purple Heart Recipient), actor, and now an author who lives in Charlotte, North Carolina.

He served several tours in Iraq during the Operation Iraqi Freedom phase, for which he received a Purple Heart for being wounded in combat. He is a graduate of Fayetteville State University (Bachelors in Criminal Justice) and Southern New Hampshire University (Masters in Justice Studies with a concentration in Counterterrorism). Clarence also pursued acting by landing roles in films such as "One Church" and the Cinemax series "Banshee." Currently, he is pursuing other avenues of entertainment that involve being behind the camera, such as directing and writing scripts for television, movies, and more books for the public to enjoy

CONTENTS

"A Children's Story"

It was a joyous day in the duck colony of the northeastern forest. The ducks were enjoying the last phase of spring. It is their favorite season of the year. They had plenty of food, along with the ideal temperatures and no threat of hunters. Winter would arrive soon, and before that, they would fly to the southern part of Florida to avoid bone-chilling winter. The ducks are migratory birds. They had to travel to avoid extreme seasonal variations.

On that day, mama ducks were trying to teach their young ducklings different flying techniques and maneuvers, which would help them fly to the south. They were teaching them at the pond so that no one got injured by falling on the ground. Gary was lounging at the bank of the pond, enjoying the sun. His friend Felix was swimming merrily in the pond. As soon as Felix came out of the pond, Gary asked.

"Hey, Fel, where are the other guys?"

Felix was the wittiest of all ducks. He always found humor in every situation, no matter how tense the situation was. Naturally, he responded in his natural sarcastic style.

"Lemme check in my pockets. Are you guys in there?" Felix looked under both his wings. "Nope, not in there, pal, sorry." He shrugged his shoulders.

"Ha ha ha, funny. I must say that your jokes would kill me one day," Gary seemed annoyed. "Let's get down to business, Fel. Is everyone ready for the trip to the south?"

"Come on, dude! Don't be so serious! I was just trying to lighten you up. And yeah, everyone is excited and ready for the trip." Felix tried to calm Gary down. "What about the elders, Felix? Are they prepared as well?" Gary inquired.

"Well, Jesse is not perfectly fit yet. Doc advised him to rest for another five to six days, but I am sure that he'll be fine till the time of our departure. Besides him, every elder is fit and ready."

Jesse was an elder duck, and he was pretty respected all around the duck colony. Unfortunately, he has been sick for the past few days, and many settlement members were worried about him. The winter was just around the corner, and they had to move out of the woods before the first snow. A sick Jesse won't be able to fly such a long distance, which was their primary concern. However, as the doctor suggested, he could fly in a few days, and that was something to cherish for the ducks at the colony.

Kelly and Rogers, the two other young members of the duck colony, were sitting on the other side of the pond. They were enjoying the sun. After all, it was only a matter of days when they would be leaving this place due to winter. They all seemed enthusiastic about their journey to the south. It was a long and challenging journey, but they had to take it every year to survive the harsh winter. As they talked about the quality time they had

spent here in the north during the springs, Kelly diverted the topic toward their upcoming journey.

"Our time over here is almost finished. I was thinking how relieved we all would be after reaching the southern part of Florida." Kelly exclaimed.

"Obviously, pal, it would be so soothing to reach there. We would be safe from the harsh winter. But, also, we would be safe from the cruelty of hunters. You know that hunting season is about to start, and those greedy hunters love to get us in their barbecue grill during the winter. So, to avoid an invite to their barbecue, we must always leave before the hunting season." Roger chuckled.

"I know, Rog. In fact, the hunters give us more trouble than the winter. We might survive the challenging weather, but we can't survive a duck shot for sure. Anyway, have you seen Benny?" Kelly asked.

"Yeah, he went to check out his ailing Grandpa. You know that the doc has advised him to rest for a few more days, and Benny is seriously worried for him. He's trying to help his grandpa recover so that he can travel with the whole flock." Roger explained everything in great detail.

"Oh, I see. I'll go and check on him in case he needs anything." Kelly left the pond with a worrisome look.

Meanwhile, Benny had already left for town to get some breadcrumbs for his grandpa. He was trying to collect as much as he could. Breadcrumbs would give some strength to Jesse, his Grandpa. Benny wanted him to recover fully before their

departure date. His mind was filled with several thoughts, and he was genuinely worried. Suddenly, Benny heard the word hunting season from a distance. He moved closer in the direction of the sound and found that two humans were talking to each other about the upcoming hunting season. He stayed there to listen to their conversation. They seemed excited about the winter and the hunting season. After all, it was considered the time of festivity in those parts of the country. One guy was telling the other about the moving-up of hunting season by a week.

"Hey, Willie, did you know they moved up the hunting season by a week?"
"Really?" Willie exclaimed with excitement.

"Sir, yes, sir. Pull up your socks. We are going to grill a lot of ducks this season." Benny instantly thought he should get back to the pond and tell others before it was too late. Unfortunately, the moving-up of the hunting season means that they had to leave earlier than their planned date. Also, no one in the duck colony was aware that the hunting season was moved up by one week.

"Hurry up, Benny! You gotta move fast." He motivated himself. What should I do about Grandpa Jesse? He won't be able to fly early. Oh God, please help us. He was thinking of all sorts of adverse outcomes on his way back to the pond because of the hunting season that would start quite soon now.

As soon as Benny reached the pond, he shouted to gather everyone around him so that everybody should know about the

need to leave for the south earlier than planned. He saw Gary and other guys roaming in the park. Everyone gathered near him after hearing his voice.

"Hey guys, I've got pretty bad news for all of you," Benny was talking hysterically.

"Calm down, Benny. What's up? What's going on? Have you seen anything horrific?" It was Gary who tried to calm Benny down.

"What I've heard is more horrific than seeing any ghost. The hunting season has been moved up by seven days." Benny barely managed to speak.
"Are you sure, Ben?" Felix asked.

"Yeah, I am sure. I overheard two humans talking about it in the town. I was there to collect breadcrumbs for Grandpa Jesse." Benny explained.

"Benny, it would be so painful for you if you're trying to play a prank on us," Kelly said sternly.

Benny was a known prankster. Kelly wanted to make sure that Benny was serious. "I am not lying. I heard it myself, Kelly. Believe me!" Benny emphasized.

Everyone looked worried after hearing this. There was a brief silence in the park.

Finally, Gary spoke, "We gotta tell everyone about it. Spread the word, Roger

. We need to pack up from here."

"Everyone, spread out and inform the others, but please do it calmly. No need to spread any panic!" Roger announced loudly.

Garry turned toward Benny and said, "Benny, you should go and check on all the elders. I want to know their status immediately. And Kelly, you should go and try to gather some more information about the hunting season. Let's meet tonight to plan the further course of action."

They all disbursed hurriedly to execute their assigned tasks.

As decided, everyone was gathered at the chosen meeting area outside the lake at night. There was a lot of noise in the assembly area as everyone was murmuring.

"Quiet, everyone! Please, be quiet," Gary shouted.

The crowd began to quiet down after Gary's announcement.

"We have an emergency announcement. There is no need to panic, though. We've got everything covered. I want you all to listen to me carefully, please." Felix started to speak. "The hunting season has been moved up." He announced.

Panic seemed to travel among the listeners after hearing this. Many worried noises were emerging from the crowd.

"Quiet, please," Gary spoke this time. "We've got an ample amount of time to leave. However, the bad news is that Jesse is not completely recovered, and he can't travel with us." Gary added.

The whole crowd looked at Benny as if they were seeing him for the last time. Some were chanting adios to Benny.

"Ok, everyone. Let's get ready to move. We gotta travel in a couple of days. The meeting is adjourned." Gary announced.

After the announcement, the crowd disbursed, leaving Gary, Felix, Roger, Kelly, and Benny to discuss the matters. "Is it true, Kelly?"

Kelly nodded in response. "I heard two humans talking about the hunt near the pond. I am afraid we need to act fast," Kelly confirmed.

"Without me, of course," said Felix. He turned toward Felix and continued,

 "I cannot let you do this on your own. I am staying."
"Me either…I am staying too," Gary shrieked in.

"Then I guess you guys leave me with no choice. I am in too," joined Roger.

"Woah, Woah, Woah! Are you guys sure about this? Because if you are, then I am in too," expressed Kelly.

They all were looking at Benny now. The curve on his face had finally lifted, and he was thankful for being blessed with such thoughtful friends. "So, what's the plan then?" inquired Benny.

"Hmmm, first, what we need to do is get everyone out of here as soon as possible," said Gary, walking back and forth with his wings on his back.

Benny nodded to that thought and replied, "Meanwhile, I will go and check up on Grandpa Jesse."

"Sounds good. The rest of us will go and check on others. We need to evacuate this pond as soon as possible," Kelly advised.

Everyone agreed with each other and disbursed once again to perform their assigned tasks. Benny rushed down the pond and made his way to the tall surrounding grass to check up on Grandpa Jesse.

"Grandpa Jess, how are you feeling now?"

Grandpa Jesse jumped with excitement when he saw Benny. "Hey Benny, I am strong as ever," he replied. Before Benny could say anything, Grandpa Jesse started coughing badly.

"Grandpa Jess, you need to sit down and rest," Benny shouted. He rushed toward Grandpa Jesse and helped him back to bed.
"I will get you some water."
"Benny, I am fine," assured Grandpa Jesse. He drank the water and asked,

"Now, what's that I hear about hunting season moving up?"
Benny was startled by how fast the news spread. "Yes, Grandpa. It is true. The guys are making sure that everyone is ready to make the trip this early," Benny confirmed.

"Well, then I better start getting ready," said Grandpa Jesse, trying to get up from his bed.

"No, Grandpa. We are staying with you until you are rested enough to make the trip."

"We? Who is we? Nobody has to stay with me because I am leaving when everyone else leaves," Grandpa Jesse stated.

"Grandpa, you are not strong enough yet," Benny argued. The concern for his grandfather was evident in his eyes.

"What makes you think I am not strong enough? A cough here and there doesn't make me weak," Grandpa Jesse argued back.

"Grandpa, I know … but …" before Benny could complete his words, Grandpa Jesse interrupted him, "But what?"

"We had so many delays during the last trip because you were not strong enough, and you flew too early," Benny confessed hesitantly.

"And you don't want to go through the same thing again," Grandpa assumed. "No, I don't. That's why you're going to rest until Doc or I say you are strong enough. Only then will we leave," Benny confirmed.

All the ducks were getting ready to start the trip to the south. Gary was preparing the group by briefing them on some of the obstacles they might encounter along the way and what was to be on the lookout for.

"Hey, listen up, everyone! Please…" Gary spoke. "I know we are leaving earlier than planned, so there are a few things I need you all to look out for on this journey."

"What do you mean?" A voice came in from the crowd.

"Yes, what do you mean? We never had to look out for anything before," another voice pierced through the crowd.

"Well…" before Gary completed, Felix took over, "Because some of us need to stay behind."

Everyone in the crowd started to mumble.

"Everything is going to be alright… Everyone, stay together and get there safe. Good luck," Gary announced.

Following Gary's words of encouragement, all the ducks started to fly away in flocks while the crew stood behind and looked on.

Meanwhile, the humans were gearing up for the upcoming hunting season. "Well, we got a couple of more days on our hands," said the first hunter.

"Yeah… Just need to get these cages loaded, and I'll be ready," said the second hunter, loading the truck with dog cages.

"You haven't got that stuff done yet?" The first hunter interrogated.

"Nah, I have been trying to get it done all day," the second hunter replied, still loading the truck.

The first hunter laughed hysterically. "I did mine the day I found out hunting season had changed."

"Hmm. I will be ready soon. I think the first stop should be down at the pond area," the second hunter replied.

"Yeah, it seemed like the prime location to get started," the second hunter agreed with the other.

The guys were gearing up to start their journey south along with Grandpa Jesse. "Grandpa, how are you feeling today?" asked Benny.

Grandpa Jesse jumped energetically. "I feel great, grandson! When are we leaving?"

"I am not sure. Gary and the other guys went out for a little while," said Benny. "Well, they need to come back as soon as possible," said Grandpa Jesse, gearing up for the flight.

"Grandpa, please sit down and rest. You need to rest and reserve your energy," stated Benny, trying to help him back to bed.

"I am fine, grandson! You need to stop worrying," Grandpa Jesse replied.
"I just want you to be strong enough to make the trip safely, Grandpa. You are the only family I have, and I will do whatever it takes to make sure you are safe," Benny confessed his concern.

"Why haven't you started your own family yet?" pried Grandpa Jesse. "It is time, Benny. I am not going to be around much longer."

"Don't say that, Grandpa," shouted Benny.

There was a sudden silence between them. Grandpa Jesse walked and played some music on an old music box he had by his bed. He sat with Benny and looked at their reflection in the water, listening to the lyrics.

Of Life Son...
We Live and We Die...
Tears rolled down Benny's face as the lyrics circled his ears.
But Through You
And Your Family, I Will
Live Forever, We Will
Live Forever
Fade Out
Gary and the others returned from reconning the area before deciding to take the journey to the south.

"So, what is the plan now that we know everyone is planning on starting here tomorrow?" Felix asked Gary.

Gary thought for a while, then replied, "We must leave here tonight to avoid running into these hunters tomorrow."

"Tonight, why tonight?" Kelly shrieked in the conversation, not paying attention to the conversation until Gary mentioned leaving the pond.

"Because we need to avoid running into these hunters tomorrow," Roger spoke the words in Gary's beak.

"Hmmm, we better start prepping then. Tomorrow is going to be a long day," said Felix, expecting the guys to agree with him.

"You are right! This trip is going to be a long one," Gary agreed.

Of Life Son...
We Live and We Die...
Tears rolled down Benny's face as the lyrics circled his ears.
But Through You
And Your Family, I Will
Live Forever, We Will
Live Forever
Fade Out

As they were talking, Benny walked up to them. "Hey, guys! So, what's the plan?" Benny asked.

They looked at Benny. "Hey, Benny! How's Grandpa Jesse?" asked Roger.
"I think he is ready to go," Benny replied hesitantly.

"Well, we know that… but how is he with making this trip?" Gary sarcastically asked.

"Well… I think he is going to be fine. However, he still needs rest, but he won't listen to me," said Benny.

Gary smiled. "Okay, good! We are leaving tonight, so we can get a jump on these hunters," announced Gary.

"Okay… so the plan is what?" asked Felix.

"I will go on ahead to scout out some rest areas," Kelly assigned herself a task.
"Okay, great! We will meet about 20 miles south of here, so be careful! The rest of us meet here tonight!" Gary instructed.

"20 miles south?" confirmed Kelly.

"Yeah, at the no-hunting zone in the next town," Gary told Kelly.
"Okay, got it! " Kelly replied.

"Okay, everyone, let's go and get some rest. We have a big journey ahead of us," Felix recommended.

"Yeah, I could use a few hours," Roger agreed.
"See you all tonight," Gary said goodbye to everyone.

The same night, everyone was peacefully asleep. The mellow moonlight was pouring down at the pond, reflecting its light to the sky adorned with millions of stars. However, the peace didn't last for long when they all heard a disturbance in the lingering peace.

Hysterically, Felix woke up and looked around nervously. "Gary? Gary?" He whispered.

Gary yawned as he woke up. "Go to sleep, Felix. We have a long day ahead," Gary told Felix.

"You hear that?" asked Felix.
"What? Roger's snoring?" Gary asked unwittingly.
"What? No! Listen…" replied Felix.

The hunters were walking near the pond, and their conversation was loud enough to create an echo.

"This pond had been known to have a few ducks around it," said the first hunter.
"Yeah, I have heard the same. Maybe we will get the jump on them today," the second hunter replied.

"I sure hope so," the first hunter wished.

"Did you hear that, Gary?" We have to get the other guys…," whispered Felix. "Wake Roger."

Roger was soundly asleep. The echoes of his snores were mixing with the echoes of the hunters. He was making a smacking sound with his beak. "What? What?" Roger woke up confused.

"Sssshhh...! We got company," whispered Gary.
"Let's get out of here," said Roger.

"No, wait. Let them pass first," said Gary.

After the hunters passed, Gary, Felix, and Roger arrived at Grandpa Jesse's hut, where they informed the others about the hunters near the pond. "We must go!" said Gary.

"Wait, what? What is going on?" Benny asked!
"The hunters are here," Felix told Benny.

"Here? Where? Here?" asked Benny.
He had just woken up from sleep and couldn't understand what they were saying.
"Yes, here, Benny. Where else?" said Roger.
"Where is Grandpa Jesse?" asked Gary.

"I am right here. Where else would I be now when I have heard about the hunters?" Grandpa Jesse emerged from the darkness.

"Grandpa, we have to leave now… the hunters are in the area," Benny told Grandpa Jesse.

"Well, if we are going to leave, then let's get to it. We must not waste any more time," Grandpa Jesse recommended.

"I am with Grandpa on this. What are we waiting for?" Felix agreed with Grandpa Jesse.

"Okay, let's prepare to leave then! But we better do it quickly and quietly," announced Gary.

30

Soon, they all snuck out of the area, away from hunters. After taking off for flight, the hunters spotted them and began to shoot at them, nearly hitting them. As they flew through the clear night sky, they tried to avoid the hunters, dodging bullets and looking for a place to rest.

"Hey, guys! We have to find somewhere to rest," Benny said what everyone else had in their minds.

"Rest… who needs rest? I feel great," said Grandpa Jesse, looping in the air. "Wow… he doesn't look like he needs much rest," Felix joked.

"We all need a break, and we will stop just ahead as soon as we get to the next town to meet up with Kelly," said Gary.

"Well, it shouldn't be long. There is a clearing up ahead," replied Felix, flying ahead of everyone.

"Yeah, I see it… we got to come in fast to avoid hunters," articulated Gary. "Hey! That's Kelly," Roger suddenly shrieked.

As they dived at high speed, shots were fired at them, barely missing them until they arrived in the no-hunting zone, where Kelly was waiting for them.

The next day, the other group of ducks was resting peacefully about 60 miles from their arrival point.

***

"Good morning! Oh, what a beautiful day it is," Felix greeted.

"Felix… Why are you Gipper? It is entirely too early," replied Benny in a harsh tone. He sounded angry.

"Benny's right… get some rest," Gary chimed in.

"It is not even daylight! Give me a break and go to sleep, Felix," Roger shouted. "Fine… you guys don't have to be that harsh," replied Felix. "I will go back to bed."

A few hours later, mellow sunlight poured down through the ominous clouds, and the guys were beginning to wake up.

"Guys, I am sorry about earlier. I am just too ready to get to the destination," Felix apologized.

"Well, next time, wait until the sun comes up," Roger replied. "Amen to that… Now, let's get ready to fly. We have a long journey ahead of ourselves," said Gary.

"Grandpa, how did you sleep? Grandpa? Grandpa? Hey guys! Grandpa is gone!" Benny hysterically shouted his concern.

Immediately, the gang dispersed, running around, looking for Grandpa Jesse. They searched the area thoroughly and couldn't find him until he caught them off-guard.

Grandpa Jesse walked in on them from behind and asked, "What are you guys doing?"

"Grandpa! Where have you been?" shouted Benny.

"Cool your feathers… I was just taking a look around," Grandpa laughed.

"You should have let someone know where you were going," Gary participated in the conversation.

"I don't need a babysitter. It is you guys who need a babysitter," Grandpa remarked.

"Grandpa! We just want to make sure you are okay and safe," assured Benny.
"Yeah, we want everyone to get there in one piece," said Felix sarcastically.
"If you guys are done, then is anybody going to dictate what time we are leaving?" bellowed Roger.

"Well, we wait till lunch before we take a flight. By that time, hunters may be a little tired," Gary took the lead.

"Hmmm, good thing, Gary," said Felix.
"Sounds like something we did to the hunters years ago," Grandpa remarked.
"Okay, so let's relax and rest up until lunchtime," Gary ordered, ignoring what grandpa had just said.

As the guys began to rest, Grandpa Jesse took a stroll to himself, beginning to show signs of being exhausted. He was thinking to himself: This isn't as easy as I thought… As he rubbed his aching wings against each other, he continued: I don't want to let my grandson down, but I also don't want to slow them down. He paced back and forth and came to a halt by sitting down to rest.

After a few hours, when the sun shone above them, the guys began to show up, preparing to leave. "Where is Grandpa?" asked Felix.

"Here he comes," said Benny, looking at him walking toward them.

Hey, Grandpa. Are you okay?" asked Roger.

"Never better… When are we leaving?" Grandpa responded.

"Well, the hunters should be worn down by now… We will be leaving shortly," replied Gary.

"Grandpa, are you ready?" asked Benny.

"I was born ready," Grandpa chuckled.

"Alright, gather around, guys!" Gary clapped his wings. He had a serious look on his face. "This is the next stop we will be making before we get to the others and the most dangerous."

While shaking his head in sorrow, Felix said, "Yeah, I remember that stretch from the last trip we made. We need to make sure we are all looking out for danger and each other."

"Well, if it is so dangerous, why do we fly this way?" interrogated Roger.

"It is the shortest route, and besides, we have to experience taking the other route. So, let's just prepare to go," Gary replied.

Roger nodded and positioned himself to take flight like the others. On a count of three, they all flew as fast as they could, flapping their wings ferociously. They flew through the thick clouds, following the river that led them to their destination.

However, their journey was not as simple as it seemed. Suddenly, shots were being fired at the group rapidly, and the group was trying their best to dodge them. "We have to fly higher," shouted Roger.

"If we go higher than this, then we will expose ourselves to more danger," replied Gary.

"What do you mean?" Roger argued.

"We might hit an airplane or something," replied Gary.

"We got to do something because Grandpa cannot take much more of this," shouted Benny.

The shots were getting closer to them, and grandpa was getting tired of dodging. "Grandpa, go higher!" Benny shouted.

"I am afraid I cannot, Benny. The shots are too rapid… Ah," Grandpa screamed. "Grandpa!" Benny bellowed.

"Gary! Grandpa has been hit," informed Felix.

"I will try to get him," replied Roger.

"I am coming for you, Grandpa," shouted Benny.

"Benny, you need to go back. It is too late now," said Grandpa.

"Grandpa! No…." Benny cried.

"Benny, I love you," Grandpa uttered.

Soon, grandpa disappeared into the forest trees below, and the guys continued to fly on. However, they were sad, not feeling the same excitement without him. "Grandpa, I am sorry," Benny whispered to himself as a tear rolled down his cheeks.

"I tried, Benny. I tried. I tried, but I couldn't get to him in time," said Roger in an apologetic tone.

"Guys, we have to get it together. He would want us to make it… Now, we fly higher," Gary commanded.

As they flew higher, the shots began to fade in the distance because they were too high up for the ammo to reach them.

Grandpa was brushing through the trees, looking for somewhere to land. "Uff, Uff, Oww…coming through." Through the branches of the trees, he made his way to the ground, though it was a hard landing. "Ufffff…" After the dust cleared, he tried to get back on his feet. "Awww… Awww…," he howled in pain. As much as he tried to get back on his feet, his pain forced him to the ground. He was half knocked out when the other animals began to come out to see what all the noise was about.

"Who is he?" A squirrel asked.

"He has been shot. Give me a hand," a raccoon replied.

"We have to hurry before they come looking for him," shouted the squirrel.

On the other hand, the hunters were sure they had hit something. "I know I hit him. He is around here somewhere," the first hunter said.

Their dogs were barking and sniffing around as the second hunter spoke. "Find him, Rex."

However, the animals were aware of the danger Grandpa Jesse was exposed to. "I will cover the scent so the dogs cannot find him," said the skunk.

"What is that smell?" asked the first hunter, covering his nose.

"The dogs will never find him with this smell." The second hunter said.

"Woo Wee… I believe you are right. Let's get out of here."

While he was still knocked out, the animals all talked and agreed to take Grandpa Jesse to Bill's house so he could rest and recover there. Mr. Bill laid an injured Grandpa Jesse on his bed and began to wipe his head with a damp cloth.

"How is he?" asked the worried squirrel. He could sense that Grandpa Jesse did not look too well.

"He's doing better, but I just hope he comes around soon because he needs to eat something to get his strength," answered Mr. Bill, who was not standing near Grandpa Jesse's head.

The next second he said that, Grandpa Jesse started to open his eyes slowly. But waking up after that terrible fall drained too much energy out of him.

"Ooooooo, oohoo ... My head, oohoo," he moaned in pain. "W-wh-what happened?" He asked, completely unaware of the tragedy that had struck him. "You had a terrible fall."

"Fall?" Grand Jesse confirmed as he rubbed his head and got up. He began to walk forward when Mr. Bill's voice stopped him.
"Hey, where are you going? Just relax..."

Alarmed, Grandpa Jesse looked back over his shoulder between the squirrel and the raccoon when he groaned. "Oh no... I can't relax," he shook his head, "I have to go," he widened his eyes in fear, "the hunters, the hunters..."

But Mr. Bill was not going to let an injured Grandpa Jesse flee.
"Wait a minute, wait a minute...." He tried to grab Grandpa Jesse gently to settle him down, "You are safe here," he assured Grandpa Jesse in his calm voice, but grandpa did not look too convinced. Instead, he looked at Mr. Bill and squinted judgingly.

"And who are you?" Mr. Bill posed a question and introduced himself, "I'm Mr. Bill, and the only place you are going is right back to bed..." he said as he held Grandpa Jesse and took him back to bed.

"Trust me, you're in no shape to do anything," said Mr. Bill, and to his surprise, Grandpa Jesse obeyed and lay back in the bed.

For the next whole day, Grandpa Jesse rested, and Mr. Bill and his friends took care of the wounded Grandpa. They cleaned

him, watched over him, and stood by his side for hours and hours when once again, Grandpa Jesse flung open his eyes.

"He's starting to come around now..." Mr. Bill announced to the rest of the gang, so they all could circle around him. "How are you feeling?" He whispered quietly in Grandpa Jesse's ear.

"Like I was hit by a truck... What happened?" He questioned as he looked at Mr. Bill's face in search of an answer.

"Well, you passed out, and you've been asleep for the last 24 hours... We thought you weren't going to make it, I mean, with all the countless injuries you suffered…."

Grandpa Jesse looked at his wing and the rest of his body. There were bruises and marks all over him. He stared with half his jaw open.

"Don't worry. It looks worse than it is." Mr. Bill could see that Grandpa Jesse was starting to freak out, so he decided to calm Grandpa Jesse down.

"Well, how come I don't feel like it," he frowned. He expected to feel better by now, but the reality was different.

"Just get some rest, and we'll talk about it later."

On the other side of the adventure, all the guys flew in complete silence after losing Grandpa Jesse. Everyone was sad. They could still not believe they had lost Grandpa Jesse, but they had to keep going.

"Benny, I know it's hard losing someone you love, but you get to keep living," Felix assured. He was the first one to speak.

Gary, too, joined him. "Felix is right; we have to keep going because we all have others ahead depending on us."

"And besides, Grandpa would've wanted it this way," pitched in Roger. He hoped his words would help uplift a gloomy-looking Benny, but they just confused him. "What do you mean?" Benny questioned.

"What he means is, Grandpa Jesse wanted you to keep living to carry on the family name," Kelly explained, and Benny nodded his head slightly.

"I guess you guys are right," he murmured, still feeling disheartened by his adoring Grandpa's absence.

He looked at the clear blue sky above him and whispered to himself.

Grandpa, I'm going to make you proud.

He was talking to the sky above him when he heard more gunshots go off. And so they all headed away from them – the hunters. If they wanted to survive, they had to fly away into the clouds.

"Guys, we've got to stay as high as possible," Gary announced as he began to flap his wings. "Now come on, let's fly," he ordered all of them.

Back at the hut where grandpa rested, the other animals were out discussing what to do about Grandpa Jesse outside when he opened Mr. Bill's door and peeked out.

"What are you doing out of bed?" questioned Mr. Bill as he looked at Grandpa Jesse disapprovingly.

"Well," Grandpa Jesse cleared his throat, "I needed to move around, and besides, I heard your voices out here."

"Well, since you are out here…" Mr. Bill pointed toward his two acquaintances, the squirrel and the skunk, and began to introduce them to Grandpa Jesse. "This is Jim squirrel and poppa skunk. They helped me get you here."

They both waved at Mr. Bill excitedly.

"Well, to be honest, we didn't think you were going to make it," Jim, the squirrel confessed.

Poppa Skunk agreed. "Yeah, you were in really bad shape."

"I've been told I was stubborn and never missed a good fight," said Grandpa Jesse with a laugh.

"I agree," Mr. Bill nodded.

"Anyway, I heard you all talking about a plan... So what's the plan?"

"Maybe we should ask you that," Poppa skunk said, staring at Grandpa Jesse.

"What do you mean?" asked Grandpa Jesse, all surprised.

"I mean, you're the only one who knows where you come from and where you're going…" he clarified as the others nodded their heads in agreement which signaled to Grandpa Jesse that he had to tell them where he had come from.

"Well," Grandpa Jesse opened his mouth. "My colony was on its way south of Miami toward a no-hunting zone, and the next thing I know, I'm here."

"So you need to get south of Miami?" Jim Squirrel asked, and Mr. Bill interfered. "That's not going to be easy since hunting season is about to start for all of us."

"Speak for yourself, Bill, because I am never in season," interrupted Poppa Skunk, and where he may be right about never being in demand, Mr. Bill was right about the other thing, which was the hunting season. Because of that, going back to the south of Miami was a hard trip to make but a trip Grandpa Jesse desperately had to make to reunite with his affectionate grandson.

Poor Grandpa Jesse was far away from the rest of his flock now and could not see a way out. If he wanted to reach Benny, he had to take all the help he could get. He turned to Mr. Bill and spoke.

"So now you know where I need to get to; what's the plan?" asked Grandpa Jesse. "We need to pass the word along the route about what we are trying to do so we can figure a way out," Mr. Bill answered his question.

Poppa skunk chipped in, "It may take a couple of days to get any response. That's why we need to get this out right now!"

"Jesse, you need to take this time to rest because this trip is not going to be easy on you," Mr. Bill advised Jesse.

The rest of the guys, by now, had been caught off-guard by the constant firing. To save themselves, they had to hide in the trees somewhere in the northern Georgia swamp. The hunters had spotted them hiding inside. This is why they ran with their dogs on their way to the area where they thought the ducks were all hiding. All in all, it was an unpleasant day for the flock. They were already miserable because of Grandpa Jesse's supposed death, and now they were being scouted by hunters.

"They got to be here somewhere," the annoyed hunter turned to his partner.

"Yeah, I know. I hit one of them..." the other hunter nodded. His eyes were scanning all of the trees for any signs of the ducks, but he could not spot anyone.

"Go get 'em, boys, find them for us," the hunters barked to the dogs as they let them loose, and they ran off into the woods barking at the top of their lungs.

"Guys, we can't hang around here for long," Gary said in a concerned voice. He knew they could be spotted any second if they hung around here for long.

"Shhhh..." whispered Benny, who could hear the noisy sound of the dogs barking. "We gotta hide, we gotta hide," Felix babbled as he flew toward the far-off patch of daylight. He was frantically shaking.

"Felix!" said Roger, tapping Felix's head. "Calm down and be quiet," Roger ordered Felix to calm down. He was afraid that if

the hunters heard their frantic voices, they'd be spotted and killed.

Then, after a while, the barks faded away into the distance.

"Ok, they are gone… Let's get ready to go," Gary said as he took a sigh of relief, but Benny cleared his throat and said the last thing either of them expected, "I think I want to go back," uttered Benny, turning very white.

"Go back?" Roger turned at once to Benny. "Why on Earth would you want to do that?" Roger was in shock when he heard Benny speak. He could not believe Benny wanted to go back to the place where they almost died. The journey back was not only dangerous but also life-threatening.

"Yeah, Benny, what's wrong with you?" Felix chimed in.

"I want to look for Grandpa Jesse…" expressed Benny, beginning to cry again, "We didn't even try to save him."

"Benny," Gary came close to Benny and comforted him, "I know you feel like we could have done more, but we had no choice but to keep going."

"But we didn't even try…." Benny tried to pull himself together as he turned to Gary.

"We had no choice!" Felix stated, suddenly looking up with a very sharp expression at Benny. "Did you want to die too?" By now, Felix was yelling at the top of his lungs. He could not understand how Benny could think that going back was a good idea.

But Benny was not going to hear any of it. "No!" Benny protested, as he started to cry, "He depended on us." He continued to cry as all the other guys tried to console him.

In the forests of South Carolina, Grandpa Jesse was being helped by the forest animals to get back to his colony in Miami. The water and blues of Miami, coupled with the verdant pinks and greens, waited for him anxiously.

"Hey! Wait a minute. Slow down… what is the daggum hurry? I only have two legs, and I don't run… I fly dog-on-it," Grandpa Jesse protested as he coughed just a little before Mr. Bill could answer him.

"Well, it is obvious that you can't fly, you old coot. Now, let's get a move on!" responded Mr. Bill as he went on.

Poppa Skunk was moving along. "He's right. We have to keep moving. The rendezvous point is a few hours away," he said as he kept walking, increasing his pace.

"Wait, wait, what rendezvous point?" inquired Grandpa Jessie as he struggled to catch up.

Mr. Bill started to laugh immediately. "You didn't think we were going to take you all the way, did you?" He said, still chuckling.

Poppa Skunk joined in the chuckle and laughed along. "We have to rendezvous with others in our circle, and they will get you to the next point," he shared. "Yeah, we told you this wouldn't be an easy journey. You see, it is more than just us involved," Mr. Bill added.

BhoO

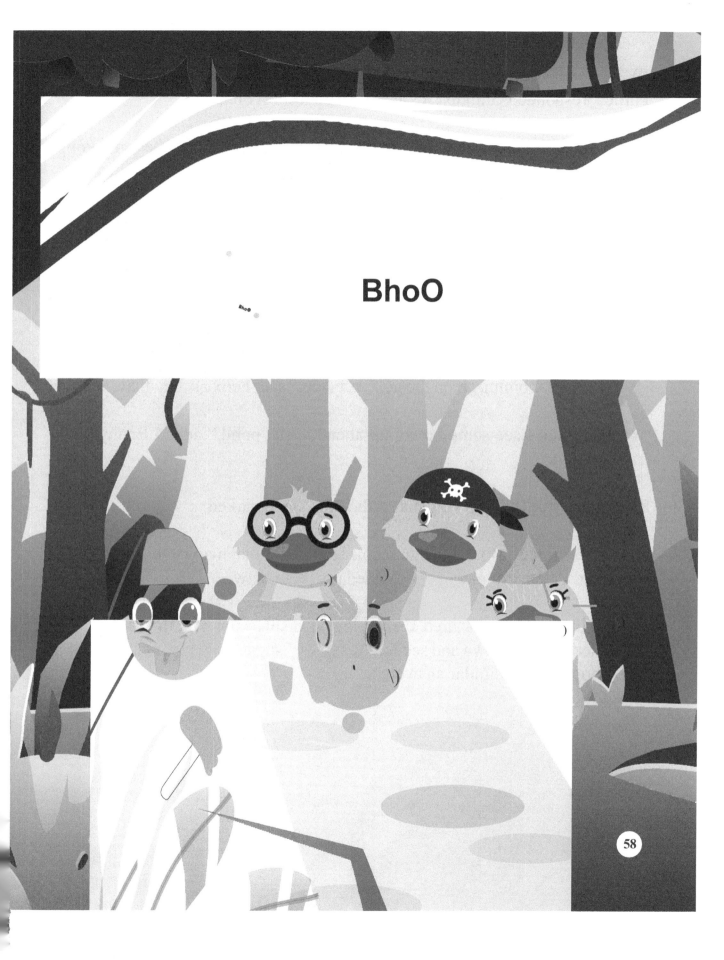

"Well, if you all are sacrificing your lives for me, I guess I can be passed around a little," responded Grandpa Jesse as he took a short break.

Poppa Skunk chuckled. "A little, let us just say you have only begun," Poppa Skunk said.

"Well, just get there safe and unharmed," answered Grandpa Jesse immediately with a smile on his face.

Later, on the state line of South Carolina and Georgia, Gary and others were getting close to their next rest stop, where they were to encounter hunters wanting to trap them off. One of them was bound to get caught alive.

"We should be coming up on the next rest stop," said Felix as they flew.

"Yeah, I think I see some others up ahead in the pond," added Benny to the conversation.

Roger intruded. "It is not very many, though," he remarked.

"Looks like three or four, but that seems strange for that many to be there," Gary expressed as Felix immediately decided to talk in between.

"I don't like this…" he shared, displaying his displeasure over the situation. "Well, let's just go down and see for ourselves," suggested Gary as he looked at Felix, hoping for a similar answer.

They flew down, but as they began to land in the water, they noticed that the other ducks were not real. Not real at all! Gary began to yell out of confusion and a tad bit of craze.

"Keep flying! Keep flying!" He shouted.

There were loud sounds in the back. All of them turned back and were looking to hear what happened while also rushing. It was the hunters! They had started shooting. All the guys couldn't help but fly in an utter state of panic, and then a net flew out. Before they could know it or do anything about it, Felix was captured.

"Felix, look out!" Benny yelled out to the best of his abilities as he saw Felix fly into the net.

"Noo!" cried Gary out of helplessness as Roger saw them frantically and added, "Oh no, oh no, oh no, oh no! Why?!"

"Guys! Help Me!" Felix yelled as the hunters carried him away into the forest, talking about the meal that they were going to prepare with the duck.

"Guys, we gotta follow them to see where Felix is being taken," said Gary.

The guys double-backed and flew high in order to follow the hunters to find out where they were taking Felix. They really wanted to help Felix out.

Later, around their camp, the hunters were planning to eat Felix as a meal. "Yeah, woo! Let's put him over there in the cage!" The first hunter excitedly said.

"He'll make a nice meal for us this evening!" added the second hunter.

"Can't wait to put him in my belly," said the third.

Felix looked scared and continued to make a noise, hoping that his guys would hear him from somewhere and somehow. All the guys flew over. Gary and the guys sent a message to let Felix know that they were there.

"EEW" yelled Felix as he covered himself with his wings. He peeked from under his wing, and poop hit him in the face. The poop was the message!

"Oops, sorry!" said Benny. "You did that on purpose," fumed Felix as he continued to clean up the mess on and around him.

Gary flew lower to look for the hunters. He heard them talk about what they were going to do with Felix.

"I can't wait to taste that duck," said the first hunter as he laughed.

The second hunter looked in the refrigerator and the cabinets. "Well, you may have to wait a little longer," he stated as the third hunter turned back immediately. "Huh? What's the problem?" The first asked.

"We have nothing to cook with, and there is no seasoning for the duck!" replied the second hunter with shock and displeasure.

"Who's making the store run?" asked the second hunter.

The third hunter immediately grabbed and rattled the pots. "I'm cooking!" He claimed as the second hunter started to scrub the knives together. "I'm doing the cleaning and cutting!" He added.

The first hunter had no choice but to be the one to go.

"Hurry back!" said both the other hunters simultaneously as they laughed.
The first hunter walked out of the door.

"How did I get doped into this? You're gonna pay for this, you stupid duck!" He spat. Felix quacked a couple of times as if he were making fun of the first hunter. "Stupid duck!" said the first hunter as he threw a rock at Felix, but Felix ducked. The hunter got in his truck and drove off.

The other ducks flew over the truck and sent some dropping down on the windshield. Moments later, in the forest near Central South Carolina, Grandpa Jesse was still on the move, being led by other animals to link up with his colony in Florida.

"I don't know how much of this I can take. My feathers are so ruffled from this forest," he said as he was being led through the forest.

Jim Squirrel immediately answered, "Well, better your feathers be ruffled by the forest than the gunshots from the hunters!"

Grandpa Jesse was blowing and breathing hard. "Shh. Can we take a break? I need some water." He paused to catch a breath.

"Oops, sorry!" said Benny. "You did that on purpose," fumed Felix as he continued to clean up the mess on and around him.

Gary flew lower to look for the hunters. He heard them talk about what they were going to do with Felix.

"I can't wait to taste that duck," said the first hunter as he laughed.

The second hunter looked in the refrigerator and the cabinets. "Well, you may have to wait a little longer," he stated as the third hunter turned back immediately. "Huh? What's the problem?" The first asked.

"We have nothing to cook with, and there is no seasoning for the duck!" replied the second hunter with shock and displeasure.

"Who's making the store run?" asked the second hunter.

The third hunter immediately grabbed and rattled the pots. "I'm cooking!" He claimed as the second hunter started to scrub the knives together. "I'm doing the cleaning and cutting!" He added.

The first hunter had no choice but to be the one to go.

"Hurry back!" said both the other hunters simultaneously as they laughed.

The first hunter walked out of the door.

"How did I get doped into this? You're gonna pay for this, you stupid duck!" He spat. Felix quacked a couple of times as if he were making fun of the first hunter. "Stupid duck!" said the first hunter as he threw a rock at Felix, but Felix ducked. The hunter got in his truck and drove off.

The other ducks flew over the truck and sent some dropping down on the windshield. Moments later, in the forest near Central South Carolina, Grandpa Jesse was still on the move being led by other animals to link up with his colony in Florida.

"I don't know how much of this I can take. My feathers are so ruffled from this forest," he said as he was being led through the forest.

Jim Squirrel immediately answered, "Well, better your feathers be ruffled by the forest than the gunshots from the hunters!"

Grandpa Jesse was blowing and breathing hard. "Shh. Can we take a break? I need some water." He paused to catch a breath.

"Water? Who needs water when your life is on the line?" said an irritated Jim Squirrel.

"If I don't get some water, I want to have a life to put on the line!" Grandpa Jesse rebuked.

Mr. Bill knew what to say, "We're almost at the next meet-up point. There is and should be plenty of water for you."

Grandpa Jesse was relieved to hear that. "Well, let's keep it moving because I need this wing checked." Grandpa Jesse and the other animals arrived at the next meeting spot to hand Grandpa Jesse off to the next group on his journey South.

70

"Water? Who needs water when your life is on the line?" said an irritated Jim Squirrel.

"If I don't get some water, I want to have a life to put on the line!" Grandpa Jesse rebuked.

Mr. Bill knew what to say, "We're almost at the next meet-up point. There is and should be plenty of water for you."

Grandpa Jesse was relieved to hear that. "Well, let's keep it moving because I need this wing checked." Grandpa Jesse and the other animals arrived at the next meeting spot to hand Grandpa Jesse off to the next group on his journey south.

"Are we there yet? Hey? Slow down! Are we there yet?" Grandpa Jesse, more yelling than asking.

"Almost. Just a little more, and we should be there," Poppa Skunk answered.

Mr. Bill intruded. "But we can't slow down because we probably got hunters on our tale," he said as he ambled forward.

"Hunters?" asked Grandpa Jesse with shock as well as fear.

"Yeah, it is hunting season everywhere, ya know," answered Poppa Skunk.

"Everybody, stop! Stop and listen!" cautioned Mr. Bill as dogs barked in the distance and sounded like they were getting closer to all of them.
"Wait here; I'll kill their sense of smell!" said Poppa Skunk.

"Do you really have to do that here? Woo, wee, what you put in that thing?"

Grandpa Jesse asked as he covered his beak with his feathers.

Jim Squirrel changed colors with a sickening look and passed out right there.

"Quick, we got to hide!" Mr. Bill said as they quickly grabbed the Jim Squirrel and ran to hide in a tree trunk.

"What happened?" asked Jim Squirrel as it started to wake up.

"Shh. Be quiet, squirrel!" stated Mr. Bill.

At the same time, the hunters were going behind the same dogs.

"They have got to be around here somewhere," said the fourth hunter.

"I think the dogs have their smell," responded the fifth hunter at the time.

The fourth hunter sniffed. "Oh, they smell something all right. A skunk. Woo Wee!" He spoke.

"How in the world are they gonna track anything with a smell like that in the air?"

said the fifth hunter as the dogs started to wind and whimper as they lay down with sad faces.

"Well, it looks like they are not. We're done for the day!" stated the fourth hunter as they gathered the dogs and started to walk away back to their truck.

At the hunter's campsite, Gary, Roger, and Benny were trying to figure out a plan to help Felix escape the hunter's cage. Gary, as he paced back and forth with tension weighing heavy on his shoulders, looked at the rest of the crew and let out a huge sigh. "There has to be a way to get Felix out of that cage."

Almost as if his voice had sparked something in Roger's mind, his eyes sparkled. "I got it, I got it," he said excitedly as the gang looked at him, waiting for him to spill out his plan.

Impatient, Benny looked at Roger and pressed, "Well, spit it out already!"

"One of the hunters is gone, which leaves the other two alone."

"We've figured that out ourselves, smart guy," Benny said sarcastically as he frowned.

"No, no… listen... The three of us can make it seem like there are a lot of ducks in the area," Roger explained, ignoring Benny's frown.

"Which will make the other two want to come out into the woods," Gary chimed in.

"And we'll go free Felix while they are gone," Benny completed the plan.

Gary smiled, fully approving of the plan. "To make this successful, we gotta hurry before they all come back," he said, and the gang all nodded.

In the woods outside the hunter's camp, the guys began to quack, so it would sound like there were a lot of ducks in the

woods. At the hunter's campsite, the two hunters immediately heard the ducks in the distance.

The second hunter raised his eyebrows as the sound of the quaking ducks began to grow louder. "Hey... You hear that?" He asked as he looked at his partner, who seemingly picked up the same sound.

"Do you mean those ducks?" The third confirmed.

"No... The grasshoppers out back..." the second snarked with a flush of temper, "Of course, the ducks, you idiot!" He rolled his eyes.

"Hey, wouldn't it swell if we had more ducks when he got back," the third hunter said as a smirk took over his face.

"Now that's using your head for something besides a hat rack..."

"Let's go," the other hunter said as the two rushed to grab their guns and ran deep into the woods where the sound was coming from.

Meanwhile, Gary had already started on his mission of freeing Felix while the others were causing a distraction.

"Come on, Felix. We have to hurry...." Gary whispered, but his eyes flashed with impatience.

Felix nodded, but then, realizing there wasn't anyone else but Gary, he pulled back in fear. "Wh- where's Benny and Roger?" Felix questioned.

"They'll meet us shortly," Gary said as Felix stood there free and ready to fly away from the camp.

"Let's go," Gary said as he took a flight so they could meet up with Roger and Benny.

"Meanwhile, at the base, the other hunter was arriving back. Where is that Dog-on duck?" He said, talking to himself as he walked toward the door of the cabin. "Hey, y'all started without me?" He paused as he spotted an empty campsite, "Where'd everybody go," the hunter scratched his head, wondering why there was no one.

The first hunter was unaware that these two hunters were walking out of the woods in search of ducks that were just not there.

"Oh shucks… we just wasted our time," the second hunter groaned. To see no ducks anywhere annoyed him enough to have his voice tighten.

"Well, it was you smart guy who heard ducks..." the third hunter said, studying his comrade carefully.

"I think you're losing your mind…." The second hunter rolled his eyes, hearing this baseless accusation. "Will you just come on..." the second hunter added. He was too tired to defend himself and argue. So, they just walked back with their heads lying low.

"Well, guess who's back? It looks like he's got a head start," the third hunter mused as he looked at the half-opened cabin door.

"Yeah, I see. The duck is also gone," the second hunter announced as he looked at the empty cage hanging there.

The two hunters thought the first one had freed the duck to cook him. They thought the duck's absence meant he was inside with the first hunter, but no delicious smells were hitting their nose. And that made the second outer scrunch up his nose to get a whiff of something... anything.

"But I don't smell anything cooking," he said as he looked at the third hunter doubtfully.

The two hunters were just about to open the door when the first hunter slammed open the door simultaneously.

"Hey, where's the duck," he asked as he tried to look in their hands to see if they had the duck.

"We thought you had it." The two hunters widened their eyes in surprise.

"Um, I don't have it," he shrugged his shoulders, and that made the third hunter's eyes bulge out of his sockets. He pushed everyone out of the way and ran to the kitchen to look at the stove. As soon as he was inside, he found himself blinking in the absence of a duck.

"You are playing, right?" He said as he looked at the empty stove. There was no sign of any duck nearby.

"How could two grown men lose one duck...?!" The first hunter exploded. "A bird that was in a cage... in a CAGE?" The hunter continued, still a little puzzled.

They all stood on the porch with their hats in their hand as they shook their heads in sorrow. And as if things weren't already bad, a few moments later, Gary and the other duck flew back over them and pooped on their heads.

"Oh — oh — oh!" The hunters exclaimed as they rubbed their heads in disgust.

In the woods, Grandpa Jesse was still on the trail with the other animals who were all trying to get him to Florida safely.

"Now that's the way to get rid of whoever is on your trail," Grandpa Jesse remarked, and Poppa skunk nodded in agreement.

"Yeah, sometimes I can get a good one-off."

"Next time, please, just give me a heads-up..." Mr. Bill the Raccoon said, jumping up and feeling rather frightened.

"I totally agree... Now let's keep moving," Grandpa Jesse said as he began to go his way forward.

"He's right; we have a little further to go."

Grandpa Jesse, with helpers by his side, started to walk in the woods, where the landscape and seasons changed every few miles.

"We must go as quietly as we can," warned Bill the Racoon. "The woods are a hunter's favorite place. I've seen many a campsite there in my days. Even some of the trees are filled with them."

At this, everyone threw a few suspecting glances around to see any signs of any hunter nearby, but all they picked up on was silence.

"Do you know your way from here, Jesse?" asked Mr. Bill, looking at the way that laid in front of him.

Grandpa Jesse looked very hard between the trees and could just see in the distance a patch of a neighborhood that he recognized. "Yes," he said excitedly, "I can see the duck colony from here.

"Thank you… thank you so much," said Lucy, shaking him heartily by the hand. If Grandpa Jesse could dance right now, he would. That's just how happy he was to see his home.

"And I do hope you will not forget us," said Poppa Skunk as he lifted a brow that made Grandpa Jesse laugh.

"I will never forget you guys… You are the reason I am back home!"

"Farewell, Jesse," said Poppa Skunk. "Will we see you again?"

"Of course! Of course!" said Grandpa Jesse, "I will come and visit with the boys. I want them to meet the people who helped their old and helpless Grandpa Jesse. Goodbye now…"

He started to run toward the far-off patch of daylight where he could see his duck colony. Grandpa Jesse, even at this age, ran as quickly as his legs would carry him. He didn't care about anything. As he ran under the pale blue sky he felt his heart

filling with happiness, and all at once, he found himself jumping at the same campsite where the whole adventure had started. He came there, paused, and looked around, panting for breath.

That's when his old ears heard the voices of the others near the campsite. It was Benny. He could hear Benny as clear as day.

"I'm here," Grandpa Jesse shouted breathlessly.

Meanwhile, Felix, Gary, Benny, and Roger had got to the campsite of their colony. They assumed that Grandpa Jesse was shot down on the trip.

"We… We…" Benny started to grow very red in the face as he tried to recall the horrifying story, but he hardly knew what he was trying to say, so he burst into tears.

"We lost Grandpa…." Roger completed, tapping his shoulder. Then, as all of them shared their story of Grandpa Jesse, they heard a familiar voice coming from a few feet away.

"I am here," the voice echoed, and all of them stared at one another.

"Is that…?" Benny said, tapping his head.

Yes, it was… It was Grandpa Jesse! The boys turned around, stunned and excited to see him. They could not believe their eyes.

"Grandpa!" Benny yelled out as he almost jumped on poor old Grandpa Jesse, but he didn't mind. He was just happy to see them all again. All the others started to snuggle in as well.

"Do you know," said Felix, catching his breath. "We really thought you had died," Felix completed his sentence after a great deal of bustle and cheering.

"No, no," said Grandpa Jesse, laughing, "I was just badly injured."

"But how did you make it back here?" Gary asked.

The other boys looked at Grandpa Jesse in anticipation. Then, he began to tell them the greatest story of his life, and the boys all listened with their eyes widening and their jaws dropping. They looked at Grandpa Jesse in awe. They were impressed by how he had made his way back to be with them.

"Grandpa, we are so sorry all of this happened," Roger apologized.

Grandpa Jesse patted his back. "It's okay, little one. You were afraid, and look, I am alive and healthy."

A moment later, all of them, Grandpa Jesse and the ducks, were holding each other and dancing round and round for joy and celebration. This was the love Grandpa Jesse had come back for. This was the love the ducks had for him. This was the journey south.

THE JOURNEY SOUTH

"A Children's Story"

About the Book

Family, life, survival, and love, will they all prevail. A colony of ducks is enjoying a beautiful day of teaching their young how to fly and maneuver the skies at the end of their summer vacation. Within hours, they learn that hunting season has moved up by one week (7 days) which gives them less time to prepare for their trip. The journey south takes them at least three days to complete, but with an elderly duck (Grandpa Jesse), the journey can be rough if he has not rested enough. They know that Grandpa Jesse needs more time to rest before he can make the trip safely. Several ducks within the colony decide to stay behind to ensure that he has enough rest to make the journey south. Will any of them make The Journey South?

About the Author

Clarence Alvin Harris is a retired Army Soldier (Army Veteran/Purple Heart Recipient), actor, and now an author who lives in Charlotte, North Carolina.

He served several tours in Iraq during the Operation Iraqi Freedom phase, for which he received a Purple Heart for being wounded in combat. He is a graduate of Fayetteville State University (Bachelors in Criminal Justice) and Southern New Hampshire University (Masters in Justice Studies with a concentration in Counterterrorism). Clarence also pursued acting by landing roles in films such as "One Church" and the Cinemax series "Banshee." Currently, he is pursuing other avenues of entertainment that involve being behind the camera. Also, he is creating a writing career in television, movies, and more books for the public to enjoy

Clarence A Harris

Clarence A Harris

THE JOURNEY SOUTH

SOUTH

"A Children's Story"

Clarence A Harris